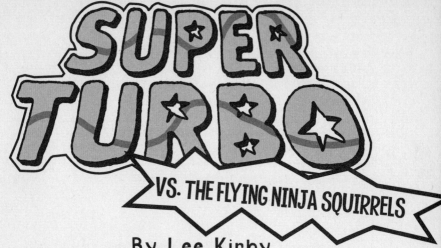

SUPER TURBO

VS. THE FLYING NINJA SQUIRRELS

By Lee Kirby

Illustrated by George O'Connor

LITTLE SIMON

New York   London   Toronto   Sydney   New Delhi

LITTLE SIMON

An imprint of Simon & Schuster Children's Publishing Division • 1230 Avenue of the Americas, New York, New York 10020 • First Little Simon paperback edition December 2016 • Copyright © 2016 by Simon & Schuster, Inc. All rights reserved, including the right of reproduction in whole or in part in any form. LITTLE SIMON is a registered trademark of Simon & Schuster, Inc., and associated colophon is a trademark of Simon & Schuster, Inc. For information about special discounts for bulk purchases, please contact Simon & Schuster Special Sales at 1-866-506-1949 or business@simonandschuster.com. The Simon & Schuster Speakers Bureau can bring authors to your live event. For more information or to book an event contact the Simon & Schuster Speakers Bureau at 1-866-248-3049 or visit our website at www.simonspeakers.com. Designed by Jay Colvin. The text of this book was set in Little Simon Gazette.

Manufactured in the United States of America 1116 MTN 10 9 8 7 6 5 4 3 2 1

Cataloging-in-Publication Data for this title is available from the Library of Congress.

ISBN 978-1-4814-8888-4 (hc)

ISBN 978-1-4814-8887-7 (pbk)

ISBN 978-1-4814-8889-1 (eBook)

CONTENTS

1

THE GOLDEN ACORN

Actually, *below* these walls, in the basement. Specifically, in the pantry. Normally, Sunnyview Elementary was filled with kids and teachers and all the things that make up a school. But it was after hours. Everyone was at home or asleep. And not a creature was stirring, except for a— What is that? A mouse?

"Fellow rats!" cried a small, fuzzy creature with huge ears and long whiskers. He addressed a crowd of other creatures just like him. Although he was a bit smaller than

the rest, his whiskers were lon-
ger. This is why he was called . . .
Whiskerface!

"I suppose you're all wonder-
ing why I called you here tonight!"
Whiskerface continued.

There was a chorus of whispers.
"Uh, was today Taco Tuesday?"
asked a tiny voice from the back.

"No!" roared Whiskerface. "It's
not even Tuesday. It's Friday!

"As you all know, the Rat Pack recently suffered a defeat at the paws of the pampered pets of Sunnyview Elementary." Whiskerface stroked his whiskers as he reminded his Rat Pack what had happened.

A team of classroom pets had showed up in his cafeteria and halted his plan to take over Sunnyview Elementary and, eventually, the world!

"But as your fearless leader, I have taken steps to make sure that the Rat Pack won't be defeated again!" Whiskerface cried.

As he said this, a couple of Rat Packers approached Whiskerface's podium, carrying what looked like a box covered with a blanket. The crowd murmured excitedly.

Whiskerface waited for the sounds to die down. "Have you all heard of . . . the Golden Acorn?!"

THE GOLDEN ACORN?!
THAT'S THE SACRED SYMBOL OF NUTKIN!
NUTKIN AND HER FLYING NINJA SQUIRRELS!

"Exactly!" yelled Whiskerface. "And according to legend, the Golden Acorn gives great strength and speed to its owner! And I . . ." Whiskerface paused dramatically, looking around the room. "I am now in possession of the Golden Acorn!"

The room buzzed. Everyone wanted to know how Whiskerface had stolen the Golden Acorn.

"I defeated the ninja squirrels in combat," Whiskerface declared, describing the epic battle.

"And now I present to you . . .
the Golden Acorn!" Whiskerface
cried. He dramatically pulled off
the blanket.

The room fell silent. Finally, a
voice from the back called out:
"Uh . . . , Whiskerface, sir . . . The
acorn . . . It's—it's not there."

Whiskerface gasped. "It's gone!" he screamed. "Someone has stolen the Golden Acorn . . . again!"

RETURN OF THE SUPERPET SUPERHERO LEAGUE

Meanwhile, in Classroom C of Sunnyview Elementary, Turbo was running his daily laps on his hamster wheel.

Who is Turbo, you ask? Turbo is the official pet of Classroom C. It's a responsibility he takes very seriously. But there is a lot more to Turbo than just that.

You see, Turbo is not just a classroom pet hamster. Turbo is also . . . a superhero! As the heroic Super Turbo, he fights a never-ending battle against evil. And Turbo *himself* recently learned that he is not alone! All the classroom pets of Sunnyview Elementary are superheroes.

Not very long ago, Super Turbo and the other pets had teamed up to prevent Whiskerface and his Rat Pack from taking over the school and then the world! After that, Super Turbo and his friends had decided to fight evil together. And they would fight it as:

THE SUPERPET SUPERHERO LEAGUE!

Turbo was lost in thought when two faces suddenly appeared at his cage.

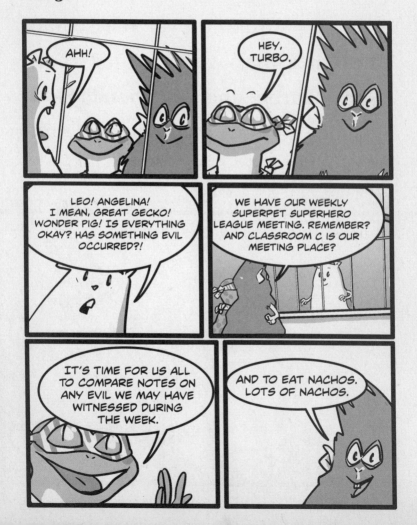

Turbo *hadn't* remembered. But he was excited to see the rest of the team, hear about their solo adventures, and of course, eat some nachos. And it didn't make sense to go to a Superpet Superhero League meeting as plain old Turbo. He would go as . . . Super Turbo!

Super Turbo climbed out of his cage and raced down to the reading nook. That was the meeting place for the Superpet Superhero League.

The Great Gecko and Wonder Pig were already there, of course, and so was Warren, the science lab turtle.

HEY, PROFESSOR TURTLE!

GREETINGS AND SALUTATIONS, SUPER TURBO!

The cover to a vent was resting against the wall. The superpets used the vents as a secret way to travel from room to room in Sunnyview Elementary. Only Wonder Pig, with her amazing maze-running skills, knew where all the vents led.

Suddenly there came a rumbling sound from the vents. Clever, the parakeet from Classroom D—who was also known as the Green Winger—came in, pushing the Turbomobile.

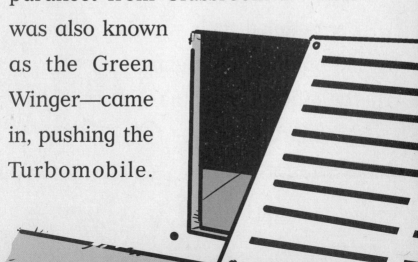

Turbo had generously given his Turbomobile to Nell—also known as Fantastic Fish. That way she could attend meetings and get around the school.

Finally, Frank—also known as Boss Bunny—came hopping in. Now, the superpets were assembled!

The Green Winger thoughtfully took notes as each super-pet detailed their week's adventures. Boss Bunny, the official pet of the principal's office, went first.

A STUDENT NAMED MEREDITH WAS SENT TO PRINCIPAL BRICKFORD'S OFFICE FOR TRIPPING ANOTHER STUDENT NAMED EUGENE.

SHE CLAIMS IT WAS AN ACCIDENT, BUT I HAVE MY DOUBTS.

MEREDITH AND EUGENE! THEY'RE FROM CLASSROOM C!

SHE'S ONE TO WATCH OUT FOR. THE WORST PART WAS, SHE REACHED INTO THE CAGE TO GRAB ME.

OOH, SORRY, BOSS BUNNY.

SHE WAS ALL LIKE, "OOH, HE'S SO OOEY-GOOEY, GAGA CUTE."

21

Fantastic Fish reported that, from her fish tank in the hallway, she noticed the janitor never locked his closet. That wasn't necessarily evil, but it was something that the superpets could look into.

The Great Gecko mentioned that Classroom A was going on a field trip next Thursday.

Wonder Pig told them how she had snuck into the cafeteria on Taco Tuesday, and that's where she had gotten the nachos. The superpets all clapped for her.

The Green Winger took a break
from writing to report that she had
witnessed no evil, but had perfected

a brand-new acrobatic routine she
was anxious to share with them all.

Super Turbo said that all was safe in Classroom C, though he did note to himself to keep a closer eye on Meredith.

Finally, it was Professor Turtle's turn to speak. Super Turbo leaned back. This would take a while. Everyone loved Professor Turtle, but he *was* a turtle, and sometimes it took him a long time to say things.

Well, that was quick! And almost as quickly, the superpets were headed to the lab!

3

THINGS GO BOOM!

The superpets raced down the vent, with Professor Turtle leading the way. In fact, Professor Turtle was moving so fast that Super Turbo was having trouble keeping up. Or maybe Super Turbo was moving slower than usual?

Probably shouldn't have had so many nachos, he thought. Then he

noticed that Wonder Pig was strug-
gling to keep up alongside him too.
And so was Boss Bunny.

The superpets exited the vent
onto one of the lab's worktables. A
brown papier-mâché mountain was
resting on the table before them.

The Great Gecko scampered up the side of the volcano and peered down the hole. "Hey, there's a soda bottle in here!" he exclaimed in surprise.

"Yes!" replied Professor Turtle. "That's where we'll be mixing our own lava! First, we need some water." He glanced at Fantastic Fish.

"Don't look at me," said Fantastic Fish from the Turbomobile. "I need all the water I have."

Super Turbo had an idea. He attached a rubber tube to the end of a faucet,

and the Great Gecko ran the other end of the tube to the top of the volcano. Using her super-pig strength, Wonder Pig turned on the faucet to fill the bottle with warm water.

"Now we need to add baking soda!" yelled Professor Turtle.

"We're going to bake a soda?!

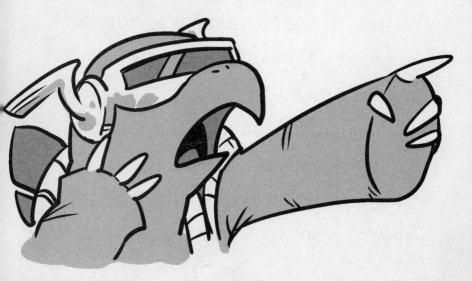

Yuck! I prefer my soda cold," said Wonder Pig.

"Not me. I don't even like soda. The bubbles go right up my nose," added Boss Bunny.

"It's too bad someone already emptied this soda bottle if we're going to need to bake it," said the Great Gecko from atop the volcano.

"Are we even allowed to use an oven without supervision?" asked Super Turbo.

Professor Turtle ran over to a box of white powder and stuck in a spoon. "This is baking soda. Green Winger, if you could kindly drop some of this into the volcano?"

The Green Winger flew the baking soda to the top of the volcano. She and the Great Gecko stirred it.

"One final thing!" said Professor Turtle. "Vinegar!"

Wonder Pig and Super Turbo carefully carried a bottle of vinegar up to the top of the volcano. They slowly turned the bottle upside down.

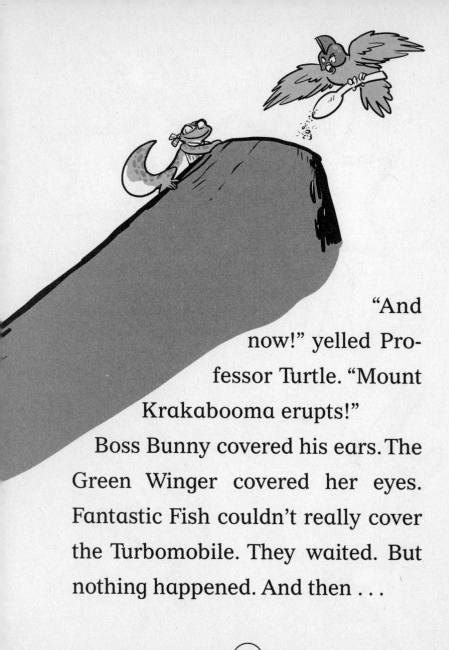

"And now!" yelled Professor Turtle. "Mount Krakabooma erupts!"

Boss Bunny covered his ears. The Green Winger covered her eyes. Fantastic Fish couldn't really cover the Turbomobile. They waited. But nothing happened. And then . . .

"Ha-ha! That was GREAT!" yelled Professor Turtle from on his back.

All the superpets were covered in lava. They agreed they should probably clean up the mess and then head back to their own classrooms to clean up *themselves*.

Just as Super Turbo was about to head back

to Classroom C, a glint of something caught his eye.

"Professor Turtle? What is that in your cage?" he asked.

"You know, I'm not quite sure," said Professor Turtle, removing his Super Visor. "It's shaped like an acorn. I found it in the school cafeteria this morning, and I was just . . . drawn to it. I've always liked shiny things."

Super Turbo tried to take a step closer to get a better view, but his paws were stuck to the floor. "Ugh, I better go wash off before I get stuck here forever!" he said. He carefully unstuck each of his paws and scampered down the vent to Classroom C.

4

AN INVISIBLE VISITOR

Safely back in Classroom C, Turbo took a shower in the drinking fountain. Then he cracked open a window to let the wind dry his fur.

It had certainly been an eventful day, even without evil to fight. Turbo was tired and he deserved a nap. But first, he had to do his patrol of Classroom C.

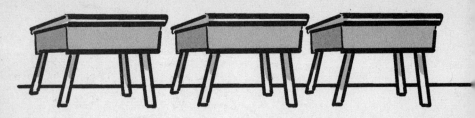

Desks all in a row? Check.

Chalk in the chalkboard holder? Check.

Hamster wheel nice and squeaky? Check.

Supergear safely stashed and drying out? Check.

Well, thought Turbo, clapping his paws together, *looks like it's all clear in Classroom C!*

Turbo pulled out his hammock and settled in. He lay back, and just as his eyes began to close . . .

Turbo sat upright in his hammock. He could have sworn he saw . . . something. A shadow. He scanned the room from his cage. *No, I'm just tired and my eyes are playing tricks on me,* he decided. He lay back down. And then . . .

Again! This time Turbo was sure something was in the classroom with him. He put on his still-damp Super Turbo gear and climbed down from his cage.

Using all of his super-hamster sneakiness, Super Turbo searched the classroom.

HE LOOKED HERE.

AND HERE.

OVER THERE.

DON'T FORGET HERE.

REALLY, EVERYWHERE.

There was no sign of any intruder. He must have imagined it all. And now his goggles were fogging up, so he took them off to wipe the lenses with his cape.

Then . . .

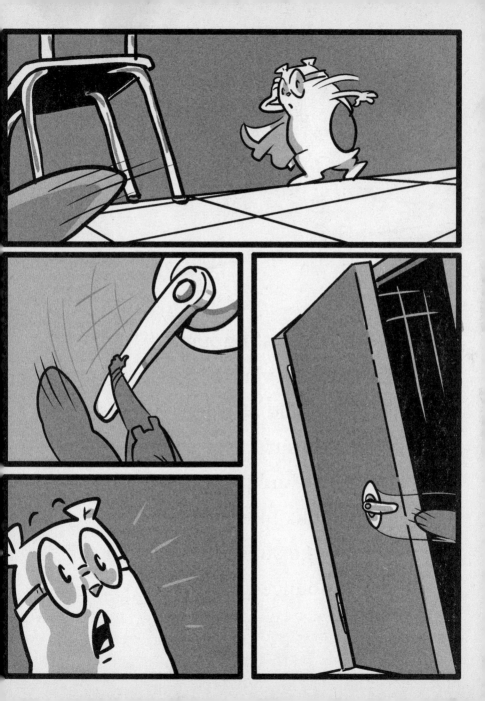

What had just happened?! Super Turbo raced over to the door. He certainly couldn't open it himself. But he was sure that someone—or something—had just gone out it.

"This looks like a bigger mystery than any *one* superhero can solve!" Turbo announced.

He ran over to the vents that con-
nected all the superpets' classrooms
to one another. He grabbed the ruler
that lay just inside the vent.

When they had formed the Super-pet Superhero League, the Great Gecko had come up with a secret code the superpets could use to communicate through the vents. Super Turbo tapped the corner of the ruler on the metal floor of the vent. The sound echoed throughout the whole system.

One tap meant: *All's well, nothing to worry about here. Carry on.*

Two taps meant: *Hey, I'm hungry. Who wants to go to the cafeteria for some snacks?*

And three? Three taps meant:

5

SUPERPETS ON PATROL!

The Superpets quickly arrived at Classroom C, ready to fight evil. Surprisingly, Professor Turtle had been first to arrive. He was usually the last, since he moved so slowly. The rest of the team followed him in.

"I'd just emptied out the Turbo-mobile when I heard the call," said Fantastic Fish.

"What's happening, Super Turbo?" asked Wonder Pig. "When I heard the first tap, I was like, oh good, all is well. But then I heard the second tap and I was like, Super Turbo is hungry? We just had nachos! And then I heard the third tap . . ."

"Well, I don't know if it's evil, but something very strange is definitely going on," said Super Turbo. He told the Superpet Superhero League what he had seen . . . or rather, *not* seen.

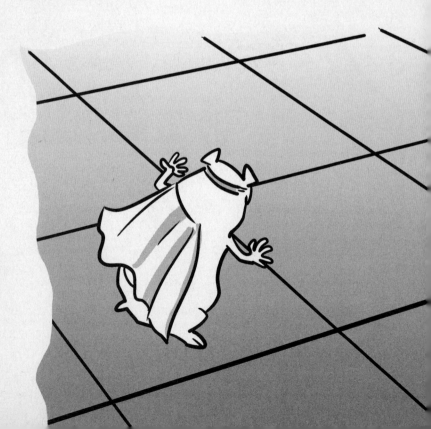

The Great Gecko stroked his chin. "You were right to sound the alarm, Super Turbo. This is very strange indeed."

"I wonder if the intruder was invisible?" asked Fantastic Fish.

"Or what if it was a g-g-ghost?" stammered Boss Bunny.

The Great Gecko was about to speak again when Professor Turtle said, "The smartest idea will be for us to split up into smaller teams and explore the school. We can cover more ground that way and meet back here in thirty minutes."

The Great Gecko blinked. "Yeah, what Professor Turtle said."

"Okay!" continued Professor Turtle. "Great Gecko: you, Wonder Pig, and Fantastic Fish can check

the hallways. Green Winger: you and Boss Bunny can check the gymnasium. Super Turbo: you and I will cover the cafeteria. Let's go, superpets!"

Everyone was so surprised by Professor Turtle's quick thinking and take-charge attitude that they stood still for a second. But it *was* a good plan, so they sprang into action.

Fantastic Fish knew the hallways the best, so it made a lot of sense for her to cover them. With the Great Gecko and Wonder Pig alongside, they were able to finish their patrol in no time. They didn't see any sign of the invisible intruder, but they did stop to lock the janitor's closet.

Boss Bunny and the Green Winger arrived in the gymnasium. Using his bunny-burrowing powers, Boss Bunny squeezed behind the bleachers to see if there was any sign of the intruder.

The Green Winger flew up to the ceiling to see if a bird's-eye view revealed some evil. They didn't find anything.

Since they had extra time, and all the extra space, the Green Winger decided to show off the new acrobatic move she had perfected: the Triple Loop-de-Loop with an Aerial Twist.

"Brava!" Boss Bunny clapped.

Meanwhile, Super Turbo and Professor Turtle were in the cafeteria. Once again, Super Turbo found he was having a hard time keeping up with Professor Turtle. But now Super Turbo was pretty sure that he wasn't getting *slower*. Professor Turtle was definitely getting *faster*. He seemed to be growing more confident, too. It was like a whole new professor!

The first time Super Turbo had been to the cafeteria was also when he'd had his first clash with evil. He and the superpets had battled Whiskerface and his Rat Pack. There hadn't been a peep from those rodent rascals since then, but Turbo gave a shudder at what a close call their battle had been. And hadn't something else happened recently in the cafeteria too?

The two superheroes completed their sweep of the cafeteria and came up empty-pawed. Nothing suspicious to be found! They headed back to meet up with the others at Classroom C.

A few moments later, two sets of beady yellow eyes peered out of a tiny crack in the cafeteria wall.

"Did you hear that? The turtle found the Golden Acorn!"

"Whiskerface is going to be so pleased when we tell him!"

6

THIS FIGHT IS TOTALLY NUTS

Back in their meeting spot in the reading nook of Classroom C, the superpets all shared what they found—or rather, didn't find—on their patrols.

Super Turbo walked away from the group and wondered to himself: *Did I actually see anything? Was that really the door opening and closing that I heard? Or was it all in my head?*

Just then, something rattled. It was the doorknob. "Guys! Look!" Super Turbo yelled, pointing.

The superpets froze as the door-knob turned, and the door slowly opened.

"Oh my gosh, they *are* invisible!" yelled Wonder Pig, and she began karate chopping the air all around her.

"They're g-g-ghosts!" shrieked Boss Bunny, and fainted into the Great Gecko's arms.

"Shh! Be quiet and hide!" said Super Turbo.

The superpets all found hiding spots in the bookshelf and waited.

After a few moments, a masked figure dressed all in black crept into the room. It didn't make a noise. It had a huge bushy tail. And it was followed by two identical figures.

Suddenly, Professor Turtle yelled out: "NINJA SQUIRRELS!"

The three Ninja Squirrels snapped to attention and took battle stances.

Their cover blown, the superpets leaped out into their best superhero poses. Suddenly, the Ninja Squirrels launched themselves at the superpets.

"They're not just Ninja Squirrels!" the Green Winger yelled. "They're FLYING Ninja Squirrels!"

The Green Winger flapped into the air as the rest of the superpets dove out of the way of the Flying Ninja Squirrels.

With her supercool Triple Loop-de-Loop with an Aerial Twist maneuver, she was able to make two of the Flying Ninja Squirrels crash into each other.

But on the ground, the squirrels were almost too quick for the eye to follow.

Even the Great Gecko, one of the speedier members of the Superpet Superhero League, was having a

hard time keeping up with the acrobatic Flying Squirrels. Surprisingly,
Professor Turtle, whose normal
fighting technique was to curl up
into his shell, was doing quite well.

The battle raged around Class-room C. Super Turbo climbed up on top of his cage and saw that the room—*his* room!—was getting destroyed! And what sort of official classroom pet would he be if he let that happen?

7

EVERYBODY STOPS

Everyone stopped and looked at Super Turbo.

"This is my classroom," he said. "And you all are really making a mess of it."

The rest of the animals hung their heads, embarrassed.

"We're sorry, Super Turbo," said Wonder Pig. Then she strolled up to the nearest Flying Ninja Squirrel, held out her hand, and said, "Hi, I'm Wonder Pig. Nice to meetcha."

The Flying Ninja Squirrel glanced back to her friends, shrugged, and held out her paw. "I'm Nutkin."

The rest of the superpets and

Flying Ninja Squirrels made intro-
ductions to one another. Super
Turbo was surprised at how polite
the ninjas were. They didn't seem
so evil, after all.

"So what brings
you to Sunnyview
Elementary, Nutkin?"
Super Turbo asked.

"We are missing something," said Nutkin after a slight pause. "Something very important to us. And we have reason to believe it is somewhere in this school."

"What are you missing?" asked the Great Gecko.

Nutkin looked back and forth to

the other Flying Ninja Squirrels. "This is a very, uh, delicate matter for us. Do you mind if we take a moment to discuss?"

"Take your time," said the Great Gecko, waving his hand. "We have some important matters to discuss as well."

The two groups moved to opposite sides of Classroom C and formed huddles.

YEAH, THAT WAS GREAT!

SWEET NEW MANEUVER, GREEN WINGER!

THANKS!

AND, WARREN, MAN, YOU'VE BEEN HOLDING OUT ON US!

DUDE, THOSE SQUIRRELS WERE, LIKE, SO FAST! THAT WAS EASILY OUR BEST BATTLE EVER!

TOTALLY!

After a few minutes, the Flying Ninja Squirrels signaled that they were ready.

"We can tell from our battle that you are honorable opponents," said Nutkin. "And because we feel we can trust you, we will tell you what we are missing. It is the sacred symbol of our clan, and we believe it gives great strength and speed to its owner. It is . . . the Golden Acorn!"

Super Turbo shot a surprised look at Professor Turtle.

"Weeeell," Professor Turtle said slowly, "I think I know where you can find that."

The Superpet Superhero League and the Flying Ninja Squirrels followed Professor Turtle down the vent to the science lab. Maybe it was because Professor Turtle didn't want to give up the Golden Acorn, or maybe he was just tired after their epic battle, but it was the first time all day that Super Turbo had no trouble keeping up with him.

They exited the vent next to the professor's terrarium. Professor Turtle slowly walked up to the cage and let out a gasp.

8

WHISKERFACE WINS!

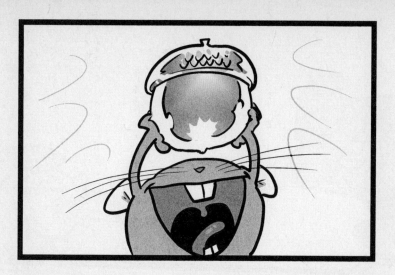

The superpets and Ninja Squirrels stared at the place where the Golden Acorn *should* have been. Suddenly, a familiar and very squeaky voice rang out. "That's right! Your precious Golden Acorn is gone!" said Whisker-face, strolling into view. "I have it!"

"Whiskerface! You rat!" yelled Super Turbo.

"Hey, Nutkin, look! It's the gold-polish salesman!" said one of the Flying Ninja Squirrels. "That's the guy who stole the Golden Acorn!"

"Gold-polish salesman?" asked a Rat Packer in the back.

"Yeah, he asked to see the Golden

Acorn so that he could demonstrate his polish. We showed it to him, and he ran off with it, all the way back to the school," said the other Flying Ninja Squirrel.

"Hey, you told us you defeated the Ninjas in combat . . . ," said another Rat Packer.

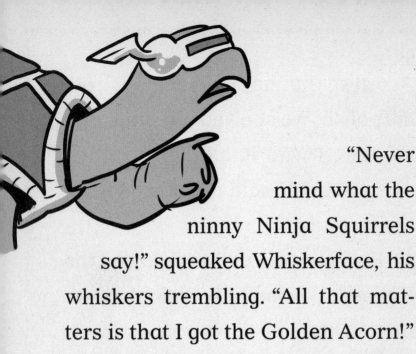

"Never mind what the ninny Ninja Squirrels say!" squeaked Whiskerface, his whiskers trembling. "All that matters is that I got the Golden Acorn!"

"And then you *lost* the Golden Acorn," Professor Turtle pointed out.

"Yes, and then I *lost* the Golden Acorn," Whiskerface said through gritted teeth. "But then I *got* the Golden Acorn again! And now that I have it, I will be *unstoppable!*"

"You're nuts!" said Fantastic Fish from within the Turbomobile. "First off, your plan is missing some key steps *again*. Second, do you really believe that acorn is going to give you superpowers?"

"Just ask your new buddies, the Flying Pinhead Squirrels! Or better yet, your old pal Professor Turtle!" Whiskerface squealed.

Super Turbo saw Professor Turtle look sadly down at the ground. Maybe his strength and speed *were* all because of the Acorn. . . .

Suddenly, Super Turbo had an idea. "Yeah, well, that's not what I heard," he said. The Flying Ninja Squirrels, the superpets, and the Rat Packers all looked at him.

"That's not what you heard, huh?" sneered Whiskerface. "Well, why don't you tell me what you heard?"

"Well," said Super Turbo, turning to face Nutkin and her squirrels. "You guys told me how you had to get the Golden Acorn back before it's too late. Before it does any more *damage*. . . ." Super Turbo winked at Nutkin.

"Damage?" squeaked Whisker-face. "What do you mean? What kind of damage?"

Nutkin stepped forward. "It's true that the Golden Acorn gives strength and speed to whoever owns it. But unless you know the secret word to unlock it, the acorn will do the absolute opposite. It will suck out any powers you already have!"

"You're—you're—you're lying!" cried Whiskerface.

Just then, Professor Turtle started to wobble.

SHOOMF!

SPROING

The Great Gecko ran up to Professor Turtle. "I can't believe it!" he said. "Professor Turtle has been drained of all his powers!"

"Oh no!" cried the Green Winger. "Who knows what will happen next!"

Whiskerface stared wide-eyed at Professor Turtle.

"You know what?" Whiskerface squeaked. "I don't want this anyway!" He shoved the Golden Acorn into the hands of the Rat Packer next to him and then ran off.

The Rat Packer squeaked in terror and passed the acorn to the rat next

to him. The game of hot potato continued until, finally, one rat handed
the Golden Acorn to Super Turbo.

Then all the Rat Packers ran
screaming from the lab.

"I believe this belongs to you," said
Super Turbo, passing the Golden
Acorn to Nutkin.

Nutkin smiled. "I knew we were right to trust you superpets."

"Are . . . they . . . gone . . . yet?" asked Professor Turtle from the floor.

"That was an impressive display of acting!" said Wonder Pig as she and the Great Gecko turned Professor Turtle right-side up.

Professor Turtle answered as slowly as ever.

The superpets and the Flying Ninja Squirrels made their way back to Classroom C. Professor Turtle was really bringing up the rear now, and Super Turbo hung back to walk with him.

"I guess . . . it really was the . . . acorn that . . . made me . . . so fast," Professor Turtle said sadly. "It was nice . . . while it lasted . . . but I guess I'm back . . . to slowpoke Warren."

"But you're not just slowpoke Warren!" Turbo said. "You're a member of the Superpet Superhero League! And whenever you put on your Super Visor, you're never just Warren . . .

○ ○ ○

Back in Classroom C, the Flying Ninja Squirrels stood in front of the same open window they had snuck in through.

"Superpets," said Nutkin, "the clan of the Flying Ninja Squirrels

will forever be in your debt. You returned our sacred symbol, the Golden Acorn. If you ever need our help, just ask. We live in the big oak tree on the playground."

And with that, the three Flying Ninja Squirrels flew out the window.

"Today was a great day!" said Super Turbo.

"Yeah, it was," said Fantastic Fish.

"We had nachos!" cried Wonder Pig.

"We made a volcano!" exclaimed Boss Bunny.

"We had the best battle ever *and* made some new friends!" said the Great Gecko.

"And I got to be fast . . . for a little while," added Professor Turtle, smiling.

"But, best of all, we defeated evil! Again!" yelled Super Turbo.

HERE'S A SNEAK PEEK AT SUPER TURBO'S NEXT ADVENTURE!

There's a new villain in the classroom. He's big, he's shiny, and he can sharpen a pencil like Super Turbo has never seen. And he stares at Turbo. All. Day. Long. But just when Turbo begins to think that the Pencil Pointer might not be that evil . . . the villain starts spitting pencil shavings! If he keeps at it, Turbo's hamster home will be destroyed. Then Turbo learns that evil isn't only trying to take over his classroom. The rest of the classroom pets are battling their own Pencil Pointers! Can the Superpet Superhero League stop the Pencil Pointers and save the school—and themselves?